FOR DAVID

First U.S. edition 2018. Library of Congress Catalog Card Number 2018940926. ISBN 978-0-7636-9688-7.
This book was typeset in Garamond and hand-lettered. The illustrations were done in mixed media.
Candlewick Press, 99 Dover Street, Somerville, Massachusetts 02144. visit us at www.candlewick.com
Printed in Heshan, Guangdong, China. 18 19 20 21 22 23 LEO 10 9 8 7 6 5 4 3 2

CANDLEWICK PRESS

ALBERT'S TREE

JENNI DESMOND

Spring arrived and Albert
woke from his long sleep.
"Hooray!" he shouted. As the snow was
quietly turning to water and trickling down from
the mountains, Albert raced to his favorite place.

His tree.

"Hello, Tree!" shouted Albert.
"I've missed you."
His tree was perfect.
Not too hard, or too soft,
or too slippery, or too prickly.

It was his own special place,
quiet and peaceful. . . .

But what was that noise?

Albert's tree was crying.

"Waa!" wailed the tree.

"What's going on?" said Albert.

"You don't normally make a noise.

SNIFF
SNIFF

You smell the same.

BOUNCE

You feel the same.

And you taste
just the same,
even upside down."

"What are you doing,
Albert?" said Rabbit.

BOING BOING BOING BOING

"Rabbit!" said Albert. "My tree is crying! How can I cheer it up?"

"Waa, waa, waa!" wailed the tree.

"When I'm sad, I dig lots of holes to play in," said Rabbit. "Maybe that will stop your tree from crying."

So Albert and Rabbit dug lots of holes.

I didn't know trees cried.

"We've dug you some
holes to play in, Tree,"
said Albert.
But the tree just kept crying.
"Waa, waa, waaaa!" it wailed.

WAA

Along came Caribou.
"What are you doing,
Albert?" he said.

What's that
noise?

"My tree is crying. I'm trying to cheer it up," said Albert. "Well, when I'm sad, I eat grass," said Caribou.

So Albert and Caribou gathered lots of grass.

WAA

WAAA

WAAAA

yum yum

"We've brought you some grass, Tree," said Albert. "Please cheer up." But the tree just kept wailing.

"Why is your tree crying, Albert?" said Squirrel. "I don't know," said Albert with a sigh.

The tree cried harder than ever.
"Pleeeease don't cry!" shouted Albert.
"WAA, WAA, WAAAAA!" wailed the tree.

"This noise is too much," said the others.

"PLEASE STOP IT, TREE," roared Albert. "STOP CRYING!"

But at that, the tree just wailed even louder .

"WAA! WAA! WAAAAAAAAAAAA!"

Then Albert had one last idea.

W A A A

He took a deep breath and
climbed quietly up to his
favorite branch. He wrapped
his thick furry paws around
the trunk and gave the tree
a huge, kind bear hug.
He whispered in his tiniest voice,
"Why are you crying, Tree?"

To Albert's surprise, his tree whispered back, "Because I'm scared of the big hairy monster."

"What big hairy monster?" whispered Albert.
"Outside, over there," said his tree.
"Don't worry. I'll get rid of it," said Albert bravely.

Albert nervously looked high
and low, outside and over there.
There was no monster.

"There's only me
here," said Albert.
"Oh, phew!" said the tree.
"I can come out, then."

A A R H !

screamed a tiny
feathered thing.
"*You're* the monster!"

A A A R H !

screamed Albert.
"*You're* the *tree!*"

"I'm not a monster," said Albert.

"I'm Albert!"

"And I'm not a tree," said Owl. "I'm Owl."

Albert and Owl laughed and laughed
at their mistake.

ha

ha

ha

They both felt *much* better.

Albert was glad his
tree was back to normal.
He and Owl played in it
all afternoon.

whoa!

whoa!

And as he watched Owl swooping from his favorite
branch, Albert knew that Owl loved the tree as much
as he did. Which, he secretly decided . . .

made his tree twice as perfect
as it had been before.